CAMILLE MAUCLAIR

THE FRAIL SOUL
AND OTHER STORIES

TRANSLATED BY
BRIAN STABLEFORD

ISBN: 978-1-943813-52-0

Contents

THE FRAIL SOUL
AND OTHER STORIES

The Frail Soul

THERE are, Monsieur, the man with the singular eyes said to me, ill-intentioned people who look at me with an impertinent pity and claim that I am mad. They will tell you that, but do not believe them; I have pronounced that word in order to destroy in you immediately the striking impression that it produces. Those people are wicked; they were my friends once, but now they spy on me and say perfidious things about me, because they are jealous. And I shall tell you with what reason: they are jealous of not having understood their soul as well as me. There are people who cannot see and who wish ill on others because of that; but not everyone can sense things in the same way, can they, Monsieur? One must be reasonable.

You have a very clear gaze; you know things; I sense that you will understand me very well and will not be astonished . . .

Monsieur, I have always been very unhappy. It is a habit that certain people acquire, I believe, at birth. I can scarcely say that from the point of view of monetary fortune, but when one knows that one is unhappy those kinds of difficulties seem unimportant. But I always found myself between two sources of mental suffering, and that strikes hard and deeply, for my sensibility became sharpened with the evil instead of being blunted.

When, as a small child, I played with little boys and girls, I was the last, or I fell, or something happened to me that never happens, and I suffered from the laughter of others more than from the accident itself. At school, I lived without comrades, having a host of ridiculous adventures, petty maladies, unjustified punishments and minuscule disappointments.

Later, I sought tenderness, of which I have always had a great need, and did not find it. Women, Monsieur, do not love sad men; and then again, it is devoid of interest to try to excite or to trouble those who had the habit of being misunderstood or bruised. It is more amusing for a young woman to take a happy man and a good talker to play that game with her.

However, I have fine things inside; I remember, yes, I had a fine, gentle nature as a young man, and I would have loved to dream and weep for long slow hours in the bosom of a woman, and I had thought so carefully of kisses, I had formed an idea of them so avid and so secret that a woman who had divined me would have satisfied, in my arms and my lips, both the soul of lust and the infantile caprice of which they are all made . . .

But they went to others.

I only found one of them who understood me; and then, it transpired that my dearest friend, who was a superior soul that I admired in loving him, fell mortally in love with the mistress that I had finally conquered. I sensed that it was her that he needed; I struggled; I would certainly never have said a word about the subject, but I could see clearly. And then, what can I say? I pushed them toward one another, so much did I feel that my destiny was to be alone.

She was delightful, but sickly; I enervated her with my feverish presence; with him, calm and solitary, I divined that she would settle down, fortified and placid. It was a better future for her than prolonging our liaison—and he was so unhappy! Finally, it was done, after months of nuances between the three of us. I was very ill. I tried to put on a distracted air, in order not to cause them too much embarrassment, but I was ill for a long time. Fundamentally, they were as good as one could desire, and I believe I acted well, above customary opinion and morality, and I remember those things with a certain self-esteem.

But that was the end; I preferred to live isolated in the future; I had endured too much. Besides which, I have never found any woman other than that one with whom life as a couple seemed possible. Until my death, if I think about it, she's the only one who appears to me. I missed her, that's all. It didn't work out, and it's no one's fault . . .

All of that is to tell you that nothing has ever happened to me, in the material sense of the word; but I've known many sad thoughts and unsatisfied sensations. I had a taste for great events, bright colors, excitements of every sort, but I only ever encountered petty circumstances, stupidities, correct and gray. Quotidian, quotidian, as Laforgue says!

I ended up telling myself that I couldn't obtain anything from my time or my contemporaries. But there was a moment when I rebelled, unable to accept that nothing at all was going to happen to me. I went out at night and harangued the trees in the boulevard like a drunkard. I remember that one of my childhood whimsies was complaining about the statues of celebrated men, because they had had the good fortune during their life to act with a precise goal in mind, and it seemed contradictory in my opinion to honor them by fixing their memory in bronze. I imagined that their souls must be suffering a great deal from that, and I said so.

It was from that idea that my first attempts at reason and empire over myself were born.

I began to think one day that I must have been going about trying to be happy in the wrong way—that there must be many people with a temperament similar to mine, and that they had doubtless been able to adapt to the life that had been made for them. Since my misfortunes were due, in sum, to trivial and everyday causes, others must have confronted them as I had and must have become accustomed to them, since they seemed satisfied. That led me to think that by looking into myself, I might perhaps find joy. Philosophers make systems to succeed in that; personally, it's by dint of being flayed by life that I arrived there without theories.

Monsieur, since the day when I began thinking in that fashion, I have been entirely happy, and it's since that same day that my friends have regarded me with suspicion, because they're jealous of what I tell them.

I ended up discerning that I was much more certain of myself than the events that had preoccupied me so much until then. And in considering the depths of my soul, I saw that it was frail, so frail, that everything there vibrated and quivered with a delightful anxiety. I could not weary of sensing it shivering, and as I studied it more, I acquired an interest in life for which I had not hoped. I became conscious of myself, I was alive, I was finally living for a goal!

I resolved from then on to devote my affection and my time to regulating the frissons of that sonorous little soul.

I began to adore it. I took it for walks while it was asleep and gradually awakened it to the sunlight. I soothed it in the shade of gardens, we conserved as good friends. I was no longer unhappy at all. Nasty people appeared to me as ridiculous marionettes. My friend and I had rare conversations. I observed from day to day that it knew a great deal and divined even more. It spoke to me spontaneously, accurately and delightfully about things and people. I've lived since then such a happy life that I don't know myself whether I haven't changed into another man.

But one evening, Monsieur, I went to see a friend that I'd met during the day, and I found his conversation so empty that I couldn't help telling him, suddenly: "My soul says all of that better than you; it hasn't existed for very long, but for its age, truly, it puts you to shame . . ."

He looked at me with a singular expression and questioned me. Then I told him everything that I've just told you; I described my little exquisite joys, my conversations with my soul. He listened to me without interrupting. I would have liked to see him rejoicing with me, but he seemed so bizarre that I bid him farewell.

I went to see him again. He talked to me again about that conversation, but in an embarrassed fashion. I was more cheerful than ever; our dialogue warmed up, and I searched for an image to give him a better understanding of the mysterious being that was living within me.

"You see," I said to him, "I think one can very well represent the soul as one represents an oriental country that one hasn't visited. Yes, I can clearly imagine the dear soul about which I'm talking. And I can see it: an adorable little girl with mauve eyes, enclosed in a crystal cage where she drums incessantly, a trifle mischievously, like the Persian lady that the giant in the tale carried on his head in a glass box.

"She's my good little friend. And every time that an impression strikes me, a dolor or a joy

that bumps into the walls of my soul, the delightful little girl plays with her little fingers on the
clear crystal, and I vibrate, I vibrate delightfully
throughout that frail soul, which is mine. For a
long time I'd felt it quivering, that crystalline
frisson, but I didn't know that it was produced
by the child's cruel and exquisite shackles, and
most of all, I hadn't seen her mauve eyes, her
crepuscular heliotrope eyes, her eyes, which are
for me the only eyes!

"Now I'm happy to be alive, and I put my
pleasure into vibrating as much as possible in
life, in order that my little crystal soul can be
joyful and chaste; and I have a companion that
I contemplate without lassitude and without
disgust, and I can assure you that I'm absolutely
cheerful . . ."

Monsieur, my friend—or, at least, I believed
him to be—took on an expression that was even
more bizarre, and he looked at me with a pity
that I sensed to be hypocritical. I divined clearly
that he was jealous, without wanting to appear
to be, and his mouth was tensed in a constrained
smile. I left him. I want to see other friends in
whom I had confidence, and they received me in
the same way. And they said strange and stupid
things behind my back.

They'll surely say them to you too, but you
can see now, can't you, that they're purely and

simply envious? Yes, yes, I sense that they can't forgive me for knowing the little girl with the mauve eyes, for not being sure that they have one themselves, and for being obliged to interest themselves in what's happening in life. I also sense that they'd like to have their little girls play with mine, but I'll never allow that. I want to have her all to myself, I don't care about anything but her, and I'm protecting her. And they can say as much as they wish that I'm an old man rendered mad by chagrin and isolation; I know full well— and you know as well as I do, Monsieur, that I'm a man of good sense. Oh, my little crystal soul, sings pretty melodies that they don't hear, my little girl has dainty fingers that they don't see, and heliotrope gazes that they don't savor!

And they bore me too much with their stories, their attitudes and their reticence; I'm going away, far away; I'm going where the sun and the flowers love one another all the year round; I'll take a great many toys, and we'll live an exquisite little life of chatter, treats and compliments, of picnics on the grass and reveries beside the sea, with my little girl with the iris eyes, with my sweet seductive little girl who sings so admirably within my vibrant, fragile and joyful crystal soul.

The Triumph in the Darkness

TO the gates and at the walls that faced the purple-tinted mountains from the height of the interior hills, the crowd rushed, pouring in thousands, arms raised and mouths open, with an immense clamor, for the trumpets, from the escarpments and the gorges leading to the city, were already singing the return of the conquest. The glitter of cavaliers suddenly shone forth among the floating banners; crowns of fire circled the roseate cupolas, the rumble of war chariots was propagated under the hymns and the cries, white horses raised up golden warriors in their triumphant capers, and the oscillating and terrible machines appeared, swayed by living waves in the gathering dusk.

The flowers of arches and porticos shed petals over helmets and furs; the host of women, perched on flag-decked capitals, threw down garlands, and the soldiers advanced with difficulty,

trailing those sumptuous bonds, which hooked
on to their arms and embarrassed their legs. Thus
appeared the first compact troops, raising luminous faces in which the sun sometimes made the
blood shine.

The prestige of the oriental evening increased
upon the victorious army the embalmed warmth
of lemon trees and aloes. Glory descended in a
great tumult from the height of the mountains
and the terraces. The plumes of archers sparkled
like multicolored butterflies; the giant reeds
of lances and long white blades developed over
their heads an innumerable and cruel flora; the
banners fluttered their fringes in the wild concert
of clarions.

The carts laden with booty displayed heaps
of florid and gold-trimmed fabrics, whose
abundance made the naked children cry out.
The immense horde of prisoners followed, four
black princes clad in silver and enchained, raised
jeers and fury with which the entire crowd was
convulsed. Pride burned in the heart of the city;
the soul of the race was uplifted, the song of joy
touched the sublime.

Finally, the parasols and smoke of incense
announced that the King of Sogdiana was about
to arrive.

In the midst of guards, his litter with arrogant
bouquets emerged, and a great void was made in

the people in the principal square, limited by cisterns.

Kneeling on the edges of balconies, clusters of young women leaned over to get a better view, and their hair was suspended, unfurling above the heads, their eyes shining between the curls.

The King showed himself, gigantic and upstanding. Steel and embroideries ornamented him like a god. The plume of his diadem quivered, a diaphanous silk veiled his face, his right hand rested on his naked sword, his left hand on the shoulder of a lord. He did not move, and his eyes could not be seen. He traversed the entire city thus, all the way to the colonnades and gardens of the great palace.

The sun was setting; it resembled an orange at the summit of the foliage; the silence that respected its decline was floating, in accordance with immemorial custom, over the people and the army. Then the King, at the top of the stairs, turned one last time toward the Occident before disappearing into the inaccessible enclosure; but it was not the supreme clamor of the triumph that saluted him at the moment when the sun sank under the earth; it was like the voice of fear itself! For the King of Sogdiana suddenly snatched away the silk that covered his face, and instead of the redoubtable eyes, two bloody holes were seen, in which an eternal night palpitated, and it was realized that he had come back blind.

Without delay, and without a word, he went into the palace, his stature effaced in a flash of metal; he was no longer visible, and the crowd broke up in the streets like the flood of a rout among the frantic gallop of the golden squadrons.

He had come back blind; in the course of the siege of the last city conquered, during the assault, the sulfur jet of a war machine had burned his eyes. But he had not wanted the return to lose its splendor; the couriers had received orders to say nothing, and, veiling his face, he had listened to the triumph in the darkness.

The King of Sogdiana did not stop in the hall where the court's feast had been prepared, and where the nobles were crowded. He commanded that the celebrations should take place as if nothing had happened. When his mother advanced toward him, distraught, he told her to be silent and follow him. And, with her and two or three young men who guided him, he headed toward the subterranean crypts where the tombs of dead kings were extended.

The place was cool and vast, silence was suspended there between the vaults, footsteps did not ring out on the fine sand, where wax fell from the lamps at intervals, allowing its fiery tears to sizzle. The blind conqueror, feeling his way, touched the steles, and the odor of funerary obscurity caressed his nostrils.

The great rumor of the feast arrived faintly through the issues that led to the gardens, and he listened, without anyone knowing what he was thinking, stopping and then walking on. He came thus to the most recent cavity, the one that awaited him—for the tombs of the kings of Sogdiana were hollowed out in advance, and the steps were already carved to take his cadaver down. He ordered that he be guided there, and his hesitant feet, one after another, slowly touched the steps, and his entire body disappeared, only his head, with its bloody and obscure eyes, emerging from the ground.

"O city," the King said, then, "I have come to confront myself here, in all my sorrow, with your joy of this evening. For now that I am blind, my place is already among the dead. What difference is there between the man who cannot see and those who can see no longer? And perhaps I have not seen any better with my eyes than I see now, and perhaps the silk of my visage does not hide any more of the life that my eyes once showed me. At present I have my feet in the place that I shall occupy lying down, and I divine that my shadow must cover it completely. At present I am beginning to comprehend and no longer to be abused, and I know better what I am. From this cavity into which I am plunged, and which goes as far as the depths of the earth, since my soul will never emerge from it again, I sense my veritable being, who awaits me, emanating solemnly. The cold breath that floats here is his breath, and the arm that I extend at random embraces his body; and it is necessary that, plunged in my sepulcher, I struggle with him and know what he wants of me, in order that, before showing myself to my people with a visage veiled until death, I know whether the veil will cover the redness of hatred, the pallor of regret or the serenity of thought. Leave me here alone with myself; let even my mother abandon me; that is my will."

And the King remained alone in the cellar, and talked to himself for a long time. He took off his armor and his diadem, and threw them down the steps. The golden helmet rang on the stone and he shivered, but did not become emotional.

The forms of darkness approached him and touched his extinct eyes, and all the dreams of death assembled, trembling, around his forehead, and he sat down on the last step to welcome them.

All night he meditated the triumph and confronted himself. He did not hear the sobbing of his mother, who, having retired to the far end of the hypogeum, considered him despairingly, so much had the charm of the blind silence penetrated him. He held himself motionless, bent over the ground, and his powerful hands crumpled his silken veil, alternately bringing it closer to his eyes and moving it away.

Toward morning, the lighter odor of arbors made him understand that day was about to break, and the warmth of the dawn reached him. His fingers seized the ash of the tomb and, filtering it, he caused it to flow over his skin. He impregnated himself with it, and touched his eyes with it, weeping.

And when he had savored the subterranean horror fully, and made the night of eternity weigh upon the temporary night of his mortal eyes, the King of Sogdiana got up again, fixed around his temples the silk that hid his hideousness, and went out of the sepulcher tranquilly, in order to climb up toward the terrestrial light.

King Cambyses

AS they approached a poor village, whose earthen huts were pink in the light of the setting sun, King Cambyses[1] ordered a halt until the following day. The horses stopped, and the archers ran to circumscribe the camp, and pikes were planted in the ground next to the carts, which discharged the slaves.

The King drew nearer, in order to supervise the establishment of his tents personally and rebuke the guards, for he feared that a murderer might enter by night, and his suspicions were perpetual.

---

1 According to Herodotus, the Persian king Cambyses II, who reigned in the 6th century B.C., died at Ecbatana in the circumstances described here, when his scabbard broke and the blade of his sword pierced his thigh. The event was, however, mysterious and other historians give different accounts, perhaps to obscure an assassination. Herodotus represents the accident as a fatal echo of his earlier killing of the sacred Apis bull during his Egyptian campaign in 525 B.C.

Having perceived a soldier leading a young woman, he called to him to stop and to bring the captive to his quarters; but the soldier, not having heard, continued walking without turning his head. Gripped by anger, the King jabbed his spurred heels into the flanks of his mount and galloped toward the man in order to seize him. But at the moment when the beast raised all four of its feet in order to jump a mount, it missed its stride and almost fell, and in the shock, Cambyses' belt snapped, the scabbard of his scimitar split, and the curved blade plunged into the prince's leg through a gap in his bronze armor.

Cambyses' scream frightened the horse, which rushed into the midst of servants and livestock, until the shadow of an ox, extended on the bright sand, caused it to stop abruptly, its hair bristling, its nostrils burning and its eyes crazed. Then people ran to free the King, who was still in the saddle.

He was livid and mute; thick blood was running over his sandal. It was necessary to lift him up with the shiny blade planted in his flesh. As the tents were not yet ready, they carried him to a building and laid him down on a wretched bed set against a bare wall where tenacious flies accumulated. The shaft of a spear was broken to shore up the miserable bed. Finally, the physicians, trembling, removed the weapon from the wound, which had traversed the leg and emerged from the other side.

The unconscious King Cambyses recovered his senses because of the extreme pain and howled with rage. Then the sentiment of fatality dominated his soul, and he calmed down. His hand wandered over the clots of blood and the bandages soaked in water, and his eyes considered the sordid wall, and he listened internally to the sound of panting life. And the sound of that life froze his soul with dread. Because he felt that he was violently afflicted, and a forgotten prophecy sprang forth in his mind, obscured by the catastrophe.

"Approach," he said to the oldest physician, "and tell me that I won't die here; for I remember that when I departed from Susa I interrogated a necromancer, and he predicted that I would end my life in Ecbatana. Undoubtedly, heaped with honors and triumphs, I shall die in my palace, a redoubtable king, amid the hair of my princesses and the standards of my guards. And here we are far from Ecbatana, a splendid capital, and this place is wretched, and Cambyses will not feel death rising to his throat in this poor hut. What is the name of this lost village where we are?"

The physician told an archer to go and en-
quire. The archer returned and whispered into
his ear; the old man became livid and shivered
throughout his body, agitating his lips, from
which no sound could emerge, while Cambyses'
sharp gaze penetrated him.

"O King," he said, finally, "it is not permit-
ted to a man to surpass himself; perhaps the
diviner was mistaken, and perhaps destiny had
whispered the true oracle in his ear. This place
devoid of beauty is not the opulent capital, but it
is similarly named Ecbatana."

"Then your cares are superfluous, physician,"
said the King, "for I sense that I shall not recover
from this blow, and that the black powers have
come toward my visage. Ecbatana will be my
tomb. My scimitar has never struck with impu-
nity; even its master will die of it. I have finished
leading my cavalries toward fertile fields, and I
shall not see my gardens and towers again. This
mud wall will be my last palace, and these blood-
stains will be my flowers, and these cruel flies
will be my musicians, since here I am, returned
to Ecbatana. For nothing can oppose the gods."

The King fell into a profound melancholy,
and when the balms poured on to the wound
had relieved his pain somewhat, he ordered
everyone to leave, and remained alone. Then he

remembered the assaults, the conflagrations, the murders and the fêtes that had edified his glory, and he lingered upon them for a long time. The plains of gilded sand, the beaches and the forests passed through his memory, until what had happened on the dazzling banks of the Nile and the giant columns of Memphis came to mind. There, setting Egyptian armies to flight, pushing before him tumultuous hordes of panicked men, he had entered as a conqueror and camped in the midst of the sacred enclosures.

There, the priests, trembling with fear, had shown him the bull Apis, the god of fecundity, the guardian of the rich country of the sphinx. And by derision, Cambyses had plunged his scimitar into it, and then had ordered that it be slaughtered and served at his table. The feast had been splendid, with an excess of monstrous drunkenness and a joy exalted by the victory. The King and his lords had eaten the limbs of the god, and like a delightful music, the sobs of a horrified crowd, heard through the bays of the banqueting hall, had delighted their souls inaccessible to fear.

At that memory, which filled his grim heart with pride, the wounded prince smiled internally. And he paraded his gaze around him, as if to seize and retain the triumphant vision on the walls. But he heard a heavy breath close to his head, and as he turned, a blue shadow appeared on the whiteness of the wall, which designed the head of a bull. The elongated image of the curved horns sharpened them like scimitars, and one of them almost touched the bed.

King Cambyses started, and although he could see, in front of him, an ox placidly passing its head through an opening, the hallucination of Apis seized him, and, crying out, he drew back his wounded leg, which the shadow brushed, and understood in a flash that the god had avenged himself. The horned shadow that had stopped his horse at the moment of the accident imposed itself on his delirious mind, and he fainted in the arms of the physician, who had come running when he heard him cry out.

When he came round, a terrible fever caused his teeth to chatter, and he had to be tied to his bed to prevent him from fleeing. His bandages had come undone and blood was inundating his garments again; and the flies on the wall, at-tracted, flew around his leg, buzzing.

The only words that the King repeated were: "Apis, Ecbatana," and nothing more was known of his obsessed soul.

Gangrene developed in the wound, the bone decayed. King Cambyses entered into dementia during his death-throes. His powerful body, hairy and brown, lay among his weapons, thrown down in the hut of white earth. The noons and nights decreed monotonously the increasing degrees of the consumption. No one dared speak; the guards avoided clinking their pikes and their swords. All that sometimes reached Cambyses' ears was the distant lowing of cattle, and as he was convulsed, unable to speak, no one knew that the sound in question plunged him more profoundly into delirium.

He remained thus for six days. Then, as the seventh morning touched the pitiful cabin with its radiation, King Cambyses opened his mouth and died. Amid the buzzing of the flies, his barbaric soul slipped away.

Marthe-Henriette

> I shall go mad
> Because, from the vine that I have,
> Another is gathering the grapes.
> (*Spanish solea.*)[1]

THE terrace of our house descended as far as the edge of the water. Opposite, on the other bank, beyond the reeds, were groves of ash trees, the image of which trembled in the current, and between the foliage, one could see fields and the edge of a forest. The murmur of the lock-gate to the left was quiet.

---

1 A *solea* is a kind of flamenco. The verse, as given in French, appears in a more recent French translation of a collection of *coplas*, a genre of love songs that became popular in the 1930s, associated in their homeland with another traditional dance, the sardana, but a more vulgar predecessor, known as *cuplés* were popular in Parisian cabaret theaters in the 1890s, often sung parodically by men in drag, and that is likely to have been where Mauclair came across them.

In the evening, a violet shadow wandered over
the landscape, and in the mist, the gilded lights
of the boats were vivid, and the eddies broke up
the reflected moonlight, or the distant flame of
burning weeds. To the right, behind the flower-
garden, a garden similar to ours hid another
house, similarly extending as far as the water's
edge, so that, by leaning over the extremity of the
hedge, whose foliage was moistened among the
rushes of the bank, one could see a little of that
neighboring garden and speak to anyone who
was there.

For a long time, the neighboring habitation
remained deserted. All through the spring and
summer I lived without paying any heed to it. I
was sixteen years old, I was suffering and silently
passionate; the aspects of nature interested me in
the most trivial details; I lived in an apparent isolation, but in reality I was never alone, so much
was I able to vary my particular conversations
with her, and mingle the joyful and the tragic in
this limited world.

One day, in autumn, I saw an old lady enter
the house adjacent to ours, and learned that she
had come to live there with her daughter, who
was nineteen. She called out to her as I was on
the threshold, and thus I learned that her name
was Marthe-Henriette.

For some time I was unable to catch a glimpse of the young woman. I was not excessively curious about her, but there was an indistinct and, all things considered, quite natural sentiment that sometimes engaged me to make the acquaintance of those new neighbors.

The ladies in question, like my parents, hardly ever went out; I did not encounter them in the neighborhood. And, when our rowing boat drifted in the direction of their garden, I never saw anyone as I passed by. I would not have been able to stop and wait without being impolite, and in any case, I did not think of doing so. Once, however, I perceived the silhouette of a slender and very blonde young woman at a window; she stepped back rapidly, but I already knew that she was beautiful, and I began to dream about her unconsciously.

Days passed. I often went out on the water. I went slowly as far as the fields on the other bank. The clumps of trees on the edge formed arbors in which a hesitant and verdant light played; little sandy inlets enclosed lucid water, colored like aquamarine, glacial and quivering. I moored there and I dipped my hands in the water or considered the vegetation living in the depths, allowing myself to live, listening to the rippling of the stream and all the fetching little noises born in solitude and silence.

One warm morning, I raised my eyes and I shivered. Marthe-Henriette was coming toward me along the bank. Immediately I named her thus internally; undoubtedly I already loved her. She came nonchalantly, without seeing me, hidden as I was in lying down.

I saw her supple figure, her naïve and bizarre eyes, her light hair, and I stood up when she was a few meters away, in order not to frighten her suddenly when she passed above me. To go back to the village it would have been necessary to go on a long way in order to reach the small bridge. I simply bowed to her and offered to abridge her route by taking her in my boat. She smiled wearily, and got in, thanking me briefly.

During the crossing I avoided looking at her; I bent over my oars, but I sensed her face in front of me. A great attractive and mute force emanated from her.

When we reached the edge of her garden, I saw that it was difficult to land; that house, having no boat, had no quay, and I had to stop at mine.

"I won't go through your house," she said. "I can easily get through the hedge." And briskly, leaning over, she passed through, waved to me, and disappeared. That was our first meeting, and I had hardly said a word.

Her memory grew within me and became more precise, was then deformed, and then came back, and I was no longer thinking about anything but her. I have never seen such a perfect and so unexpected a face; she had to think about special and rare things. I became accustomed to prowling around the hedge frequently.

One day, I went along it all the way to the end. I advanced my head and saw hers close by—very close by. She did not turn away, and looked at me; we spoke almost simultaneously. I don't know what we said, but we spoke. I can still see her mouth, fleshy and red.

After that, tacitly but with a secret will, we came back repeatedly to talk in that fashion. Sometimes, I spent entire days thinking about her mouth.

Marthe-Henriette was cold, but strangely intelligent, and she asked me what I was thinking in the fashion of an adviser and a friend. She was three years older than me, and that distance raised her up, making her already a woman relative to me. We agreed that I would take her out sometimes in the boat. Her mother, who was in poor health, was confined to her room, so Marthe-Henriette was free and alone.

We made a few excursions on the river like that. She liked and understood the water, and told me pretty things about it. She had a way of talking about it that delighted me; her soul was burning with comprehension and life. Now I looked at her without constraint, and I always encountered her simultaneously vague and in-sistent gaze, the gaze of a consciousness that was seeking and going to open up . . .

Our conversations were tranquil. I loved her with all my heart, but I did not tell her so; a thousand reasons kept the words on my lips. I was always afraid of not being understood, it was never the right time, and the difficult details of existence frightened me; I was born to be alone.

We watched the decadence of the season together. We were familiar with the declining suns whose tender sadness penetrated us with a voluptuous sensation. We saw dramas and exiles in the foliage and in the water; we were touched by the heart-rending spectacles of a nature whose beauty was fading into death. The extreme au-tumn descended over the things of the forest and the plain with an indefinable savor. My love grew more and more.

I only saw Marthe-Henriette at certain hours. Days sometimes went by without my seeing her come; she didn't tell me what she was doing and I didn't ask her. Gradually, she changed. Her complexion paled, her eyes became larger and darker, her figure more supple; she seemed weary and anxious. She got ready to speak, and then fell silent, as if waiting for something. She also showed some affection for me, but there was an increasing distance between our sentiments. She was a friend, her attitude that of a wise counselor, from which I suffered somewhat while smiling, becoming grave and very obscure.

There was an intervention in her life that I didn't understand. I knew that at that age, young women are modified throughout their being, and I attributed to that the secret movements that were reflected in her face, the fugitive nervous tremors that escaped her. Increasingly, however, I sensed the necessity of telling her about my love, whatever might happen, and that folly seemed to me to be urgent. I struggled to make up my mind to do it, while weighing the frightful imprudence of that confession. In me, too, a long-awaited maturity was becoming manifest, and I saw that I could no longer prevent myself from speaking.

I therefore resolved to tell her everything, and I waited for an opportunity. One evening, at about six o'clock, we had agreed to go out, and while I as waiting for her with the boat in a corner of the flower-garden, I swore to myself that I would be firm, and master my fear. It had been two whole days since I had seen Marthe-Henriette.

She arrived and joined me, but she was so extraordinarily pale, with a moist and happy gaze, that I was disconcerted.

"I have something to tell you, my dear little friend," she said, smiling and hesitant. "Soon, yes, soon . . ."

I cast off and we floated mutely, both gripped by presentiments. The exquisite and mysterious hour impressed us more than usual. We looked at one another, seeking to read one another's faces. I didn't know what she wanted, and she probably sensed that I was oppressed by something too. That lasted for some time. We came back, and drew nearer to the bank.

"Soon," she said. "It's a confidence so grave . . . I don't know . . . when we're on the bank, I'll tell you, but you mustn't look at me . . ."

What was it, then? A thousand thoughts went through my brain, tumultuously, haunted by hope and fear. I no longer dared to exist.

Marthe-Henriette stood up, leapt on to the ground, leaned over the hedge as she normally did in order to bid me farewell. Her eyes seemed to me to be filled with a joy, a pride, a blossoming as tenebrous as it was absolute.

And she said to me then, bending toward me,

very quietly, in a whisper, her red mouth almost touching mine: "Do you know, little friend—I have a lover!"

And she fled, swiftly. A veil covered my sight; I dropped my oars. Already she had gone back into the house, vanished into obscurity, behind the walls, behind the world.

And I, I stiffened myself against the flower-garden, crying internally, with an infinite heart-break: "Marthe-Henriette! Marthe-Henriette! Marthe-Henriette!"

Tylea

WE came, among the rocks and the purple-tinted pines, all the way to the summit of the hill. And from there, the undulating forest was revealed in its entirety. There was no one there; a gray beech trembled and the foliage let out the birds, and the decoration of the late autumn born of the mosses and obscure arbors, and the discoloration of the mist counseled the heart to a sadly fearful silence. The somnolence of the belated hour and the inactive wind left in the timid sky a few long, slow clouds. And the humid vapor trailed, suspending itself over branches with indolence and desolation.

I sat down next to Tylea and I united her with my body, with the raised flap of my cloak surrounding her little hunched shoulders, because she was cold. We didn't look at one another, but our gazes descended separately over the landscape, and we considered it anxiously. The pearly mist rose from the depths of the valleys and floated; in the distance, the wooded crests of mountains protruded their extreme summits in long cliffs of an indefinable color. Between them, vast empty spaces were reminiscent of the sea, the white mist confused there with the sky, a flora of submarine shadows effaced beneath that illusory water.

The mirage of the northern sea was surprising; between the slim back trunks of pines one glimpsed with certainty, the absence of the rumble of marine tides seemed astonishing. The sadness and cold of the North spread a bleak dampness over the country; the rocks opened caverns to the emptiness; the idea of the primal ages of humankind persisted, at a time when the deliverance from chaos still smiled so weakly. It really was an exceedingly melancholy September landscape.

And at a moment when the sentiment that everything was finished, renounced, dissolving, was intolerable to us, we turned toward one another, eyelids lowered, and our eyes gazed mutually at one another's lips, and following the gaze, our lips went to meet, half-closed over our teeth, and they touched, tasting and doubtless appraising all the warm and melting sinuosities of their design. And a savor of fog gripped us at the moment when our breath was retained in our mouths. We remained thus, in the immobility of the kiss. The coolness touched our faces; they quivered; they were only warm at the central point of the mouth that linked them together; and without separating, we pulled the folds of the broad cloak more tightly over our shoulders and backs. Tylea's frail body, in the benevolent obscurity of fabrics, modeled itself on mine; the rising wind mingled a curl of my lover's hair with my eyelashes. We came apart in order to brush it away.

"How beautiful and desolate it is here," said Tylea. "Kiss me a great deal, kiss me well."

My lips burned on hers. There was the mute, insistent and voluptuous dialogue of amour between my lips and hers. The flesh brushed and constrained, coaxing and voracious by turns, and the fruit pressed against the fruit expressed the strange juice that is good and does harm.

But we drew apart again, and I said, very softly: "Don't you sense the taste of the cold fog on our lips, Tylea?"

"Yes," she said. "I sense it in spite of your soul and in spite of mine."

"We have to go, Tylea; let's go back."

And without quitting her, without removing my cloak from our joined shoulders, I made her get up with me and we went down through the rocks.

And I said to her, in a whisper: "Kisses are no use when nature is afraid. Kisses are no use when souls have sensed the melancholy dampness of the vale and the trees. Let's go."

We came back from the hill and reached the heart of the foliage. Shady it was, and bleak, dormant in a violet-tinted vapor, and already the face was scarcely visible there, and the eyes seemed hollow; one was thin and indistinct there. And within the heart, consciousness hid, huddled and chilly, in the flesh.

Tylea started to sing to disconcert the mute beings born of the silence, and her frail voice rose up among the trees—but after a few moments she fell silent, as if fingers had made a sign in the air, and her small, poor voice expired.

And I said to her: "You're not singing any more, Tylea?"

"No," she said. "It's necessary not to sing here, I sense that."

Mechanically, I replied: "You're right. Singing is no more use than kisses when the season is weary."

And we walked without saying anything all the way to the road. Sad, long and pale, it was born from the forest and snaked all the way to the village. The first houses appeared, a thread of smoke rose up, and roseate gleams touched the windows. The oblique shadow descended over the roof; the powdery linden-tree hung over the wall, and the disjointed thresholds remained bleak.

The noise of our footsteps was loud in the deserted street. We reached our enclosure, but no one came out to meet us, and when I pushed the wooden barrier, I perceived that the room was empty. Doubtless some errand had taken the maidservant away. We remained alone in the penumbra. The monotonous ticking of the clock told its indefinable little chaplet. We sat down timidly, next to one another, tired and absent-minded, avoiding looking at one another. And nothing welcomed us more tenderly in the house than in the forest, and a confused impression of inactivity and coldness was prowling everywhere in that dusk.

And suddenly, I heard that Tylea was weeping, and a profound sigh reached me, and I saw that, lying back in her crumpled hair, the dear child of sadness was bowing her head in despair. And she said to me, convulsively, squeezing my hands:

"Oh, since we love one another dearly, why, why aren't we happy? There's an evil atmosphere

here that draws off all joy. Why must I weep without any apparent reason, as if the sobs had been accumulated in my breast by weeks of calamity? Everything is good, however, we're in the repose of a village, we're not suffering from any malaise, we're not anticipating any quarrel or accident, we've been for a walk, I've sung, I've kissed you, we're like all those who love one another dearly and who are simple. Why is there something that penetrates us with anguish? What's happening?"

And I looked at Tylea, and I said, softly: "There's nothing, there's nothing. Learn, then, that this is what is called happiness, the life we're leading. Poor weeping chills, that's all it is, happiness, nothing better has been found. And you might be defended against all material evils, but you're suffering from the autumn, and you have the sentiment of that which is going away, and that sentiment comes from the depths of the earth, and what is making you feel bad is your soul. And I too feel bad because I have a soul, and the best thing would be not to have one, because we don't understand the tragedy of the season, and our kisses would have been tranquil, and you would have sung at your ease, if the sentiment of the infinite sadness of things hadn't gripped both of us. That's what we ought not to understand, that's what causes your tears, that's what gives birth to the darling tears between your lashes, Tylea. Happiness ends where those thoughts begin, do you see?"

And the child raised her head, and her eyes shone, and, drawing me toward her, in a very low voice, a whisper, I heard her say:

"Oh, kiss me, you. For if that's happiness, I want to exchange it for the evil of understanding that you're telling me about. And when I think of the fashion in which I love you, my darling, the same tears come to me, and now I sense clearly that the happiness that makes me weep is neither beautiful enough nor large enough to fill my little girlish soul!"

Luce-Évelyne

THE blue fly buzzed, immobile in the sun-light. The violet shadow of dwarf poplars above the balustrade extended. The sparrow chirped as it hopped; everything was lucid and powdered with gold. Luce-Évelyne came as far as the convolvulus on the balcony. *I'm slow*, she said, *slow. Alas, alas! How little the sun cares about my hair, my eyes and everything that I am!*

No footsteps sounded on the sand of the pathway. The violet shade was untroubled; the latch of the gate remained mute, and the foliage immobile. In the distance, after the variegated descent of the roofs and terraces of villas toward the sea, came the descent of the hill of roofs emerging from the verdure, red, white and gilded, with their silken canopies and vases of flowers. Further away, from the white stripe of the road snaking through the dunes to the maize and honey of the sandy beaches, there was the slumber of the blue sea, the profound satin of the sea embroidered with little birds and Levantine tartans. And in the utmost background, a sky was confounded with the water, two skies, two seas, united in a hectic kiss. Over those things sang the first hymn of the paternal sun.

Oh, said Luce-Évelyne, *sun, sun, where can I be taken to be cured, since you care for me so little!*

She leaned her chin on the stone balustrade. She mingled her hair with the stems, leaves and flowers of the convolvulus. One laughed between her teeth; she bit it; but her thoughts were sad. It was a delightful morning in Cannes, at the center of the gulf, the air embalmed by lemon-trees, and the gaze extended a long way over the enchantment of the blue sea.

Playthings lay on the mats, and bleak dolls, under the gilded azure. Luce-Évelyne no longer looked at them. Since her illness and the first blood on her little handkerchief, since the cough, the balms and the voyage amid anxious faces, she no longer played. Oh, how long the train had taken to follow the gray road of the immense exile, from Paris, the mists and the electric pallor of railway stations on the evening of the departure! After long months of sadness, after the unsustainable languors in bedrooms, among the shadows, the ennui, the potions . . .

it had been necessary to go toward the sun, and
they had spoken of him as if he were a living person, like a Maman stronger than the other, wiser,
who would take Luce-Évelyne in his warm arms,
who would laugh with her, gild her frail curls,
and who would prevent the blood from redden-
ing the little handkerchief. And he was there, the
sun!

That's not a Maman, said Luce-Évelyne.
Everything was lucid and powdered with gold,
the shadow stood out clearly, mauve on the white
stones. She thought: *That's not a Maman. Alas,
how little the sun cares about me!*

The entire sea was flamboyant between the
honey sands of the gulf, like a sapphire in the
gold of a ring. The sky was radiant in turquoise.
The mountains burned, and, on the horizon, the
peaks of the immobile Alps. Birds striped the
air with their white flight, and with their white
flight, the bisquines and the brigantines striped
the water. Everything was warm and soft. The
play of the light in the foliage was marvelous.

Luce-Évelyne leaned on the balcony for a long
time, her dainty head tousled between the cold
blue volubilis. And she thought that the sun was
terrible, majestic and indifferent, that she was
too small a girl for him to care more about her
than the florets or the seashells, and, feeling that

she was so frail, she looked at her body, the little shadow it extended, the poor little thing that was her hand. And comparing herself with the toys, she felt that she was as paltry as they were.

Sun, sun, she said, *you're not kind, you're too beautiful and too big, you're to hot and too ripe. You pay no attention to me, you're leaving me all alone. I've been brought to you to be cured, but you're not putting yourself out for Luce-Évelyne. I prefer the familiar shade of my bedroom, and its softness on the portraits and the trinkets. She cares about me more. The shadow is kinder.*

And she wept.

Other mornings passed, then afternoons of glory and candor on the terrace. Luce-Évelyne was always thoughtful. Sometimes footsteps sounded feebly on the sand of the path, soft lips kissed her forehead, affectionate words soothed her, and delicate hands wandered very gently through her hair while profound eyes were reflected in her own. And in slow days of opulent light, the streaming of brightness and perfumes, there were exquisite concerns, anxiety veiled beneath smiles. Luce-Évelyne felt herself bathed in kindness, caressed with a moist suavity like milk. The poignant and adorable drama was played out between her mother and fate, at every minute, the drama with thousand details, accumulated bedclothes, displaced drapes, moved screens, shadows disposed for perfect repose, for the cure—oh, the life of the dear darling!

And when the mother, after all these precautions, imploring the supreme complicity of the august light, went away pensive toward the horizon, she sensed in front of her the invisible, inert and tenacious enemy that was only doing one thing: advancing. The slow hands of the clocks revealed its progress, and the dolorous reverie was amplified in innumerable waves, until, in the silence, the little cough complained, so sadly, in the muffling of the little handkerchief, and with a horrible surge, the mother came back—not too quickly, the expression calm—and murmured, in a tranquil voice, the "It's nothing" that was always, instinctively, on her lips, in the initial bewilderment that the spectacle of fatal things produces.

The days increased in beauty. Everything was beautiful, as if that really were an emanation of the elements, as if everything had been created for that destiny. But Luce-Évelyne became a little paler every day. She gazed at the descent of roofs and terraces toward the sea, the white terraces with their bright silk canopies and their flower vases, and she said, her delicate face framed in the convolvulus:

Sun, sun, you're wicked! You light up and warm the mountains and the sea, which have no need of it, and you don't care about me. You're too big to play with me. You pay no more attention to me than to a stone or a leaf. Oh, sun, since I've come all the way here to look for you, to be cured, kiss me and warm me a little better than the waves and the rocks, because, you know, they don't love you as much as I do.

She said:

Sun, I no longer play with my toys. You're annoying me, you scare me a little, you're too beautiful. When I began to learn, before I was ill, I read that you light up half the earth, and that's big, big! I understand that there isn't enough warmth for me, and that you don't have time to think about me.

She thought:

There ought to be a little sun just for me, a big orange of fire. You, I detest, you're too big, one can't even look at you.

And as she turned away abruptly and threw herself in her chair, she coughed in the little handkerchief, she had pink in her cheeks and her lips, and she did not say anything more.

Having fallen out with the sun, she was sad in spite of the toys, Luce-Évelyne. She became very pretty, diaphanous, unreal. She looked at her pink cheeks in a mirror. *I ought to be called Luce-Rose,* she said. *Oh, naughty little pink handkerchief!*

She played with her curls, gleaming with frail gold, and wrapped up her dolls in her bedclothes. *Wicked sun, these are my daughters, you shan't play with them, they're for me alone. Oh, if you wanted, wicked . . . !*

The violet and lukewarm shadow was unmoving. The mauve shadows were outlined on the white stones. Everything was soft, supple, spiritualized by light.

It isn't worth the trouble of talking, said Luce-Évelyne. *The light talks too much, it's just a matter of listening. I'm beginning to like the moment better when it becomes crimson in the west, when it's seven o'clock, and they take me behind the windows of the greenhouse; the same blue fly flies into the crystal, the big trees are all black. It's very pretty. Sun, you annoy me, leave me alone. You look like a big spider that takes the scenery between its yellow feet. I'm ignoring you. You're as garish as a cymbal.*

Thus entered into Luce-Évelyne's soul the prophetic melancholy of dusk. And it seemed to her that she understood the merciful meaning of nature, as she was effaced like a shadow.

An evening came, after others, when the sun leaned toward the arbors of the occident, appearing like a grenadine among the foliage, sowing precious stones over the gulf and crimson blood over the crests of the distant Alps. Luce-Évelyne was paler; she felt the cough coming, and watched the light decline over the occidental landscape.

All the same, the sun is pretty, she said. *I like you all the same. You're very naughty to me by day, but at the moment when you go away, you're nicer.*

You're nicer, stay, she said. And as the sun, at that moment, sank into the blue sea in an orange agony: *It's him, all the same, that's needed. It's always him that the world needs. But why are you leaving? It's all the same to you that I'm suffering. You're wicked.*

The little handkerchief was very pink in a little cough, almost a chirrup. And, raising her two little arms in the profound dusk, she stiffened and died, Luce-Évelyne, like a bird.

Ilse of the Geraniums

THE little cadaver was lying almost at the level of the clear water, in such a way that, as his lips were parted, his teeth could be seen shining. Above, among the reeds, the grassy slope of the dyke rose up, and the trees were already somber against the pink sky. Their identical reflections descended alternately into the canal, and the lined up, thus elevated, in a long double row on the bank, dominating the flat polders all the way to the horizon. A few traces of gold and nacre faded away in the placid dusk, and because of the great silence, the wind of the nearby sea was inert.

The dead child's head was titled back; two bunches of red flowers could be seen through the shallow water in his hands, and there were others scattered beside him. One was floating above his mouth. His face was tranquil; it seemed to have slid while sleeping over the damp grass, and not to have woken up in death. The weather was joyful that evening; the rows of trees were unmoving, and the heart of the sky opened like a fruit above the child.

Until the sixth hour, everything remained thus, and the annihilation had no witness. But at the sixth hour, a little shadow appeared, inverted in the mirroring canal, and moved amid the images of the poplars; at the end of the high dyke, a voice sang, and a little girl came from the East. She was blonde and dressed like a pauper. And on the opposite bank, on the side of the fields, a second shadow, in the inverse direction, depicted a second little girl coming from the Occident, and they advanced toward one another. This one had bare arms, her figure stiffened in a flower-patterned corset, a long blue skirt ballooning like that of an infant, and golden jewels mingled with the curls of her temples. She was a child from a fairy tale, such as one sees in the region of Zeeland.

At the moment when the symmetrical twin shadows touched at the forehead and were confused, the girl of the fields looked up toward the dyke, at the top of which, the other, a silhouette circled with gold by the sunset, looked down. And having perceived one another, they considered one another without speaking, the Zeelander a trifle disdainful, the beggar-girl hesitant, with a half-smile.

"*Bonsoir*, you," the latter finally said.

"*Bonsoir*," said the Zeelander. And after a moment, with gravity: "You're not from here, are you?"

"No," said the other, "I've come from Flanders." And immediately, she added: "You know me, I'm called Ilse. And you?"

"Me, I'm called Tine."

"How pretty you are, Tine," said Ilse. "You look like a princess."

"We're all like that here, Ilse," said Tine, flattered. "We always put on nice clothes to go see the fields. I'm from Westkapelle, over there to the right. It's past the bridge of the canal, and then further away. There's a beautiful big tower, and then the sea with shells and white birds, and big painted boats, and a blue belfry. It isn't as pretty where you live?"

"Yes," said Ilse, "it's very pretty here; that's why I ran away. I'm from Wilsele. It's all bricks, and there's a lot of smoke, and because of the coal people are nasty and all black. I wanted so much to see the water. Here, it's a garden, the houses are like toys, and there are flowers everywhere."

"Flowers everywhere, Ilse. Everywhere, and you haven't seen everything yet. The flowers grow without anyone wanting them, on the road, by chance; there are thousands of them. Look, geraniums, lovely red geraniums, there are some just below you, on the edge of the canal, I can see them. They flower without being planted here . . ."

"I'll go pick some," said Ilse. "I'd like to give them to you, Tine, but I can't cross the water, and yet it isn't very wide here, I can see your eyes very well."

"No, you have to go over the bridge," said Tine. "Go down to the bank, you can pick the geraniums before it gets dark."

Ilse went down; her silhouette went into the shadow of the grassy slope, and she suddenly seemed almost indistinct. Birds were calling. There was a silence.

"Ilse," said Tine, "can you find the geraniums? Lean over, lean over, they're beside you, a little more to the left, a little more. Look, what's that I can see on the edge? What's that in the water? I can see something just beside you . . ."

"Ah!" cried Isle, terrified.

"What's the matter?" called Tine from the other bank.

"It's a drowned child, Tine, a little drowned boy. He's half in the water."

"A little boy, Ilse?"

"Yes, yes, a little boy, he's drowned, he's dead, he doesn't look frightened, but he's dead, and he's so handsome. He's drowned on a day when they sky is so joyful, Tine! There are geraniums in his hands, and around him there are some that are floating."

"Can you see his face, Ilse? Don't look at him, you'll be too frightened."

"No, no," said Ilse, "I'm not frightened, but what are we going to do? We're all alone, and you can't do anything, there's water between the two of us . . ."

"We can't do anything. How is he, the little boy? Is he from here? Does he have golden fasteners?"

"Yes, yes, around his neck, and very blond, very long hair. He's handsome. What a shame!"

"Perhaps it's Kees," said Tine. "He's from our village. He left for the polders this morning. He went over the bridge, and he always brought back flowers. It's him, without a doubt. Someone has to come . . . it's late, I can hardly see any more . . ."

A cold breeze ran through the mauve sky; the trees were congealed in obscure masses, and the silver of the canal seemed more livid. The tall reeds were rustling.

"Go to the village, Tine," said Ilse. "I'll stay here to mark the place."

"But it takes at least an hour to go to Westkapelle and come back," said Tine. "It'll be dark, you'll be scared, you can't stay here with the dead little boy in the dark!"

"I'll stay here," said the stranger. "I'm not afraid of death or the dark. I'm not from here, me, and I've seen many things since I've been walking everywhere. The little boy isn't wicked, and the sky is going away without wishing any harm to anyone. Go, hurry, I'll stay sitting here."

"I'll go, then," said the Zeelander. "See you soon, Ilse . . . but I can no longer see you at all . . ."

She drew away. The rising shadow hid her at a bend in the canal on the opposite bank, already bathed in a blue-tinted vapor and indistinct. Ilse remained alone, sitting down, without looking at the half-submerged cadaver.

Time passed.

Mechanically, her hands played with the geraniums in the folds of her dress. The great descent of the dusk attenuated the pale pinks of the extreme Occident. The wind of the sea, increasingly sharp, curbed the grass, and a vast complicity of the solitude and the silence was decreed over the mute polders. The reflections of the trees filled up with darkness

"Oh," said Ilse, "it's getting cold."

She folded her arms and looked around. Her eyes came to the little recumbent body, and a placid pity rose up in her simple soul. The monotony of the grass wearied her gaze. Slowly, she whistled between her teeth.

Tine will be a long time yet, she thought. *The village is a long way away. Everything is very big this evening.*

She picked up her flowers and arranged them. She remembered a nursery rhyme from Flanders and sang it in its entirety, her eyes vague: "Three white lambs, three white lambs. One came from Neuzen. One came from Wilsele. But the third no one knows.

"The first went to the alderman. He gave him a silver collar. The second went to the prettiest bride. She gave him ribbons.

"But the third went straight to the church. And he lay down on the altar. With a gold cross and a great light. And they saw that he was the lamb of Paradise."

And when she had sung, Ilse looked at the dead little boy again.

"It's necessary that he doesn't look so wretched," she said. "They'll find him so wretched!"

She seemed to have an idea, and suddenly she took the child by the shoulders, awkwardly, and drew him out of the water toward her. Then she spread the petals of her geraniums over him, mingling them with his hair, arranging them around his neck and when she had no more, she picked them in the dark, with grass.

"He'll need other flowers," she murmured. "These are too small, they aren't colored enough. I don't have any. He won't be very handsome, and then, he'll also need candles, but at least he won't look so poor." She spoke very softly, and hesitantly; and unknowingly, she offended the evening and death with her insolent flowers, smiling, as busy as a housewife preparing a surprise.

When she had finished, she leaned over to see. Everything was darker; a flock of swallows fluttered over the water, quarreling, and disappeared. In the distance, in the violet-tinted mist, the flicker of a light finally became more precise, and grew, and a murmur was born. Shadows elongated between the trees mingled with the nocturnal sky.

And Ilse, tranquil, climbed up the slope in order to be seen by the visitors of death; and she watched them coming, standing very straight, and without gestures, the guardian of the obscure soul, the tragic picker not understanding the sacrilege of that ironic funeral, an obstinate statuette of Life standing in the increasing darkness next to the little cadaver, violently profaned by the red flowers.

The Evil Hour

IN the middle of the last page, Luc Deraines wrote the word *Fin* in small capitals, and below it, to the right: *Antibes, November 189*– Paris, June 189**. Then he put down his pen and looked around.

The vast study was bathed in sunlight. The English wood paneling with nickeled metal inlays was shining; very brightly a sunbeam was playing on the gilded and tawny leather of the armchairs, on the tightly-packed bindings of the bookshelves, and mirroring the polished floor. The glazed bay at the back, beneath a white blind with blue stripes, allowed a glimpse of a garden fiery with light, where tall trees cast a violet shade. Two svelte enameled vases in the room displayed bouquets of moist roses. A Claude Monet seascape framed in gold like a sapphire and a few Helleu dry-points, neat and diaphanous in their white lacquer frames, hung on the matting of the wall. The atmosphere was intimate, and deliciously calm; no noise of the city reached the house buried in a park; Paris seemed not to exist. Flies were buzzing against the windows and going away again. Suddenly, the bell of the Ursuline convent began to chime.

Luc Deraines lowered his eyes to his table. The manuscript of the finished novel was placed in the center, regular, rectangular and massive, with his title: *The Triumph*, in large letters, an epigraph from Edgar Poe, the date, and the already-celebrated signature. At present, it seemed that a great exit had just taken place, and the writer sat there with anxious eyes. The phantoms that had been haunting his brain for eight months had disappeared definitively into the pages; they were imprisoned there, and that packet of paper remained as heavy and immobile as a white cenotaph striped with funerary inscriptions. Nothing immaterial any longer escaped into the room; the writing had seized everything, and one book more was one dream less.

That singular sentiment of emptiness mingled in Luc Deraines' soul with the heavy wellbeing devoid of curiosity that comes from concluding a long and painful task, to the point of disturbing him. He stood up, lit a cigarette and started pacing back and forth in the study, astonished not to be content and light, as he had been once at similar moments.

The sentiment of ennui was definitely growing. He stopped and examined his Claude Monet, although he knew it by heart. Then he went to the window, gazed at the sunlight on the blue-tinted leaves, and followed with his eyes a caravan of dazzling clouds magnificently flamboyant in the azure. Slowly, the clouds disappeared. Deraines went back inside, wandered, absent-mindedly, and suddenly surprised himself in front of his etchings, his hands dangling, thought himself stupid, and went to sit down again.

Oh, he said to himself, *what's the matter with me? One would think that I'm in a bad mood.*

Sprawling in the armchair, he saw his manuscript, and turned away abruptly to avoid it. The feet of the chair screeched on the floor stridently, and Deraines' nerves were dolorously pinched by it. Mechanically, he extended his arm toward the pile of his preceding volumes that stood in a corner of the table. His fingers climbed up along the bindings. One, two, three novels, a volume of plays, and that thinner volume . . . oh, poems— and that stout one on top, essays. Six in all, and a collection of tales and chronicles, and the mass of paper that he did not want to look at, there, on the stand, to the left. That would make seven.

Seven volumes already! Deraines was gripped: seven volumes, really! He had thought he was still on his third.

"I'm forty-three years old," he articulated, aloud. "That's no longer such a 'young master,' as the newspapers like to say."

And suddenly, his eyes fixed their gaze on a little mirror with a lucid glass, scintillating in its steel mount. He seemed pale, the head slender and handsome, the gaze penetrating, the youth sensual and ironic, but the corners of the eyelids were stretched, and also the corners of the lips. Bistre circles made the eyes hollow, the curly hair was gray beneath the temples. A sharp and fugitive pain passed through his heart like a flash, and his complexion lost its color. That pain had definitely been recurring too frequently for some time, and the physician didn't seem to be paying any heed to it . . .

He turned the mirror away, thoughtfully.

Melancholy descended upon him somberly and pitilessly. He was alone, all alone in the world, with no true friends, but a crowd of casual comrades—men of letters, journalists with overly hasty handshakes; he wrote to distract himself, and fundamentally, he didn't care about it at all. Success had come in large measure, very quickly, to his subtle and delicate books, nuanced with passion and irony, written in a musical language, more musical than colored, more gripping than powerful. He had created a novel of mingled ideologies and landscapes, and had found that he could formulate with ease what many young men desired. He had developed, under various faces, the initial theme of his books, and now *The Triumph*, concluded, was about to summarize everything, supply all his conclusions. He would not be able to go any further; it would be necessary to repeat himself or to change. But those books were not imaginative play; it was his life that filled them, under various names—and to remake his life would be difficult . . .

Fundamentally, this last book was already in the preceding one; one could well have anticipated already all his final affirmations therein. And then, what next? What could he do?

"It's that I no longer see anything at all," Deraines confessed. "I've said all that I could say that's new. There's no hiding it, that's the way it is. Of course, I could always write pretty little complicated stories; I have an audience; they'd sell. But seriously . . ."

A regret at having finished, at having killed his life by saying everything about it, caused him to turn back to the manuscript that contained it. How grave and menacing it was, that cube of blackened paper alone and heavy on the table. It was, in sum, a testament.

"A testament? What a word! I'm not very cheerful." And he smiled, without conviction; the justice of the term struck him regardless.

"How stupid it is, literature!" Deraines murmured. "People will read my novel; I know in advance the malevolent criticism of one, the eulogy of another, who don't understand my individualistic theory at all, and then the procession of letters, people who come up to you on the boulevards, who have only read the names and one chapter, in order to be able to congratulate you without making a blunder, without confusing you with some other successful monsieur . . . pooh! There are young men who'd love all that, it's true . . ."

And he admitted, immediately, that young men were already totally indifferent to him. Forty-three years old, heart trouble, seven volumes!

"And then, they must have had enough. They'll let go of me, like the rest. What rubbish! I think I'm writing for myself, not caring about anyone else, and all the same. I have a host of ridiculous anxieties, a grotesque fear when the book comes out, discontented headaches when I see that some imbecile hasn't understood. I know full well that he's an imbecile, but I'd like him nevertheless to like what I do! How sickening!"

It was, above all, that anticipation of an abandonment, the keen sentiment of being the plaything of fashion, of risking his fearful soul and his sensibility in that derisory avatar, that sickened Deraines. One can't be sure of anything. And that ceremony of publication, with its known rituals, categorized in advance, how exasperating it was! Had he worked for months to receive for a seventh time the same articles, the same jealous or amiable faces, the same newspaper advertisements, the same grimaces of influential old baronnes that he frequented out of necessity? He was disgusted with it before going back to it. A series of disagreeable faces obsessed him, and spleen took hold of him powerfully. He opened the novel at random and read a passage.

"Oh," he said, "how weak that is! And then, I said almost the same thing in my fourth book!"

It was true. Was he beginning to repeat himself so soon, then? And was he sure that his work was on the level of the others? Was it necessary to deteriorate? Oh, no, never that! To decline, to publish less interesting things, to connect up morsels already written, to patch up ideas that were already stale! Deraines thought about the Academician Demarne. He too had made a rapid fortune with his novels of sentimental voyages; he had made his little world tour, and then the vein had run out, and for two years he had been collecting his articles in volumes, in order to have the semblance of still existing, to maintain himself; and the public sensed that he was finished, sales were falling in spite of the advertisements. What a fate!

Deraines became even more desperate—because he too had to think about making a living. In sum, he had nothing; an ease prolonged by new editions, journalism, feuilletons in the big newspapers, but all that could vanish with his fashionability, and very quickly ...

What a hidden anguish was that of the man of letters! And to be not even certain of meriting real art and real thought!

Everything was crumbling around Deraines, irremediably. It was the great crisis, finally arriving with the conclusion of that last book, which was also the closure of his life. He reread the final page, in which was formulated, with self-confident pride, the clear vision of the life accepted, the morality of energy and disdain.

Liar! Liar! he cried, internally. *If the others knew how fearful you are and how you've had enough! "Young master," they say. Master of what? Servant of their momentary hobby-horse, and that's all, and when they have another idea to amuse themselves, they'll leave you behind all alone! Self-confidence! Energy! I have to wear all that on my face, or else they don't take long to make comments: Uh oh! he looks tired, Deraines. You'll never know how tired I am, imbeciles! And to think that I've heaped up seven volumes to repeat the same thing, which I don't even think!*

And he fell back in is armchair, his head in his hands, his heart convulsed by an immense disgust. Mechanically, he muttered inconsequentially: "Oh yes, I've had enough, I've reached the end . . . nothing more, finished, Deraines . . . surrender your place, Deraines . . . you're getting old, you're lacking interest . . . you've lasted long enough, my poor lad . . ."

And tears came into his eyes, trickling coldly between his clenched fingers.

As he moved, his sleeve hooked on to the handle of a drawer, which opened. He looked into it, saw a revolver shining vaguely, and mechanically placed his hand on the butt, brought the weapon out—and all his being went toward it, that shiny, decisive, mute object.

His fingers felt the icy steel. His burning palms liked that sensation. He no longer felt anything except that coolness, and his body no longer appeared to weigh anything, no longer to exist.

The weapon was cambered, powerful and short, in good order, the breech loaded, the hammer cocked, and the trigger taut. The cross-hatching of the ebony handle dug into Deraines' skin, making it prickle, making an impression there. He could no longer see anything but that single point. His eyes became lost, his soul vanished; without trembling, he slowly raised the weapon. And as he raised it, the tick-tock of his watch in his fob pocket reached him through the fabric, more violent, more terrible and more solemn . . .

There was a sound of footsteps, the door handle creaked, and a domestic appeared at the back of the room, without seeing.

"Monsieur, there's a Monsieur here who wants to speak to Monsieur. It's that reporter from the *Instant Parisien* who came yesterday when Monsieur was out . . ."

"I'm not seeing anyone," said Deraines, as if in a dream.

The door closed.

Oh, I've finished with it; it's necessary, he thought, raising the weapon again.

But with a sharp stabbing pain in the heart, his entire life rose up; something red passed; all the energy was shattered. He stood up, plunged the revolver into the drawer with both hands, and threw the manuscript on top.

"Yes, yes!" he shouted. "I'm receiving! Come in!"

The door opened again, and a man appeared, laughing and gesticulating.

"Marvelous my dear master! I've forced the issue—too bad, I've come to see . . . but you seem to be in pain. Am I . . ."

"No, it's nothing," said Luc Deraines, effortfully. "I'm very happy to see you."

And with a vague gesture in which all of his decline, all of his acceptance and all of his conclusion were confessed, for him alone, he advanced his hand toward a chair.

"You're never disturbing me—sit down."

The Illusion

O Beloved, the best proof of love that
you have inspired in me is that
I am overflowing with amity for you.
Laforgue.

MAXIME turned his head and looked at me. Standing up, his forehead applied to the window, he had spent long minutes looking out into the garden at the tall trees rusted by autumn, his face seemingly thinner in the dusk, his hand tormenting a crease in the large satin curtains patterned with silver flowers, brushing the sumptuous cracks or mechanically pursuing invisible arabesques over the window-panes with his finger.

"Come on," he said to me, "do you think that anything is forgotten? Time passes over the events, and one makes arrangements to live anyway, to repair the damage to the human machine, to pad one's existence with apathy, but one doesn't forget . . .

"It's now seven months since Maia left for London with Jones Rey—seven months, you hear. Yes, it was when that imbecile got the medal of honor; three days later they disappeared, and I found Maia's frightful little note . . . I thought about killing myself, and very seriously, as you know, since, without your idea of taking me to Spain . . .

"She'd left me half-mad, eaten away almost to the marrow, unable to lift an item of glassware without dropping it, with the tremor of someone on the brink of paralysis. Well, I lived anyway, still with these trinkets that she loved, and this pastel signed by her. I look at that from time to time. I'm ingenious in passing the time; the great crisis is over. But I haven't forgotten anything at all. Look, I can see her in that armchair you're sitting in, I could tell you how the creases of her dress . . . And her eyes, when dusk fell in their profound pupils, lighting up the famous golden dots there . . .

"Forget? Is that possible? First of all, one wouldn't be alive is one didn't remember. It's a sign that one isn't entirely a grain of sand in the wind, that one persists slightly in one's poor being, that one holds a little place before the

scattering, the vain and filthy dissolution under-
ground . . ."

Now he was walking back and forth in the
drawing room with long strides. The bright fire
made the crystal in the dresser sparkle, set fire to
the narrow mirrors fixing their cold transparency
between the golden serpents of their frames, and
reanimated the faded gold thread of a chasuble.
Plunged in a low armchair, with a cigarette dying
between my fingers, riffling through an album of
engravings, I watched my friend.

"Well," I said, suddenly, "do you think one
can forgive, if one hasn't forgotten?"

"I don't know. It depends . . ."

"On what?"

"Listen, if Maia . . . damn it, I almost said that
I'd forgive her, and I don't even know whether I
ought to hold anything against her. She passed
through my life like a season, quite simply. I
didn't have any rights over her. She hurt me, but
is it ever someone's fault when that happens?
Everything in existence is based on the form of
horizons or the perfume of gardens, or even less
. . . No, I can't any longer render her responsible
for anything at all. Except that one doesn't like to
have nothing to forgive, because it's painful and
strange. It's as if one were trampling a portrait
of someone dead. One has a luminous phantom

of joy once experienced; if it can disappear, one recovers it; if not, how can one ask forgiveness for no longer being able to love?"

"Then you no longer love Maia?"

Maxime stopped dead, then came toward me, and, without replying, took two engravings from the open album. One was a drawing by Odilon Redon entitled *The Genie Nailed by the Ear*; the other was an old German lithograph representing a man flayed alive, dragging his skin, attached to his heels, around a room, zigzagging like the comical cadaver of a balloon.

"Listen," he said. "This is what women can do. They can take a man with bright eyes and nail him by the ear to the wall of imbecility, like that genie trying vainly to detach its own. They can lay our hearts bare and leave us to wander bloodily, trailing the specter of our life at our heels like the man dragging his skin. Can we know whether we love them or not? Couldn't Maia do with me whatever she wished? Well, yes, it's cowardly what I'm saying, I know, but I love her enough to admit it right away. I see nothing base in love . . ."

He had stood up again, and approached the pastel hanging on the wall.

"Look at this thing, one of the strangest that she signed. That oriental head, those eyes as green-tinted as an ancient pond, that hair reddened with all the magnificence of an autumn sunset, that frail neck where opals and aquamarines are dying on a golden thread, those sad sensual lips, that infinitely dolorous gaze as chaste as the immemorial snow of lost glaciers; it's really her. Maia Reni, the sorceress, the painter of specters born of the night, the celebrated and redoubted mystic, the exceedingly pale Maia that wept with me in the evenings, when I was ill . . .

"But look closer. There's a little blood on the neck, on the hair, whose redness is heightened by it, and the water around it is pink, and the head is severed: it's floating, alive, like a nymphea, among thin garlands of forget-me-nots and anemones . . . One doesn't penetrate that dream immediately; one thinks it a decorative dream, a fantasy of an artist remembering Gustave Moreau or the primitives; but at close range one sees death, and the macabre strangeness of Maia painting her own severed head. It's with that artificial love, for that severed head, that I love. She glides through my memory like a faded flower, like a venomous *Victoria regia*—decapitated, you understand— that she attracts me still, like the pale face that one cherishes as much after having divined it thus, coquettish and lugubrious, ornamented with petals and blood, *Beyond Life* she titled this pastel, and it's beyond life that my dream keeps her intact . . ."

I looked at Maxime. "I can see that you still love her."

"How do I know? I ask myself sometimes whether I don't love her uniquely in that terrible portrait. And then, why talk to me about that? Maia is so far away!"

"Not as far as you think," I said, slowly.

Maxime turned round, took a chair, sat down facing me, and said, with a feigned calm: "What do you mean by that? Has she come back?"

"Well, yes, she has come back. She's in Paris."

He became very pale, but as I was about to tell him everything all at once, to get it over with, he spoke very rapidly.

"So she's come back here? It's true? Oh, but it doesn't matter to me anyway. There's Jones Rey with her. It's annoying—we're going to run into one another in various places, inevitably. There's always hypocrisy in cold politeness, painful appearances, after that kind of quarrel . . ."

"Jones Rey won't be there, Maxime," I said, getting up. "He's in the country, near Exeter, painting a large ceiling for the Duke of Osborn."

"They've separated?"

"Fallen out. Maia has come back to Paris alone."

"You've seen her?"

"Yes, yesterday—and she even talked to me about you . . ."

"About me?"

I went to the window in my turn, turning my back, and I was getting ready to speak in a low voice, to say my piece in a rush, when I heard a noise of urgent footsteps, Maxime running after me. His hand clutched my arm, gripping me violently, and forced me to look at him, plunging the dolorous and moist gaze of his beautiful eyes into mine, making no attempt to hide the anguish that was contracting his delicate features and twisting his thin lips.

"In that case, Luc, don't hide anything from me, I beg you." His voice was trembling. "You can see that I'm in a bad way, that I'm mad. Speak—she talked about me, she's left Rey, what did she say, where is she? Has she sent you?"

"She wants to see you, she'll be here soon. Oh, she begged me. I knew what had happened, I didn't want to, but I ended up promising that I'd prepare you . . ."

"You . . ."

"Don't hold it against me . . ."

"Oh, I don't hold it against you, my dear, dear Luc! One doesn't say no to her! But, my God, what a coward I am! I had a great pain in the heart when you said . . . So she'll be here soon! I sensed what you were going to say, I wanted to press you to say it, and at the same time I interrupted you to delay it, because I was afraid of what you had to say. When will she be here?"

"At half past five. It's five now. She said to me: 'Go up before me, Deraines, I beg you. Prepare him. I want to see him, I love him . . .'"

"She said that!"

Maxime stretched himself out in an armchair, tilted his head back and spoke into the vague gloom.

"Luc, will you light the little lamp over there, on the sideboard . . . forgive me, but the idea of ringing, of seeing Gilbert going back and forth . . . we're alone, aren't we? Light the lamp near the pastel as well. I'd do it myself, but I can no longer move; I'm floating in the void. So she's going to come? If I'd thought that an hour ago I'd have believed myself demented. I told you that one doesn't forget, and I was right, that's why I find it natural that's she's coming. How little we are, even you, Luc, you're robust . . . but me! For seven months that memory has always been there. I see it when I wake up in the night, all alone. I've tried to bring other women here, but as soon as I loosen a tress of hair my fingers touch Maia's hair, and not recognizing the face, I tell the other to go away. Now she's really coming back. Deep down, I make myself sick . . . to think that that Rey, that man to whom she's a hundred times superior . . . Find me repulsive if you like, I think of that and I love her just as much. Life is bizarre and dolorous, Luc. I want to believe that yours is simpler . . ."

"Don't believe it, my friend . . ."

"Oh, I know that you've been there too. All our sentiments of that time are mingled . . . But tell me, will she really come? Are you sure? Yes—your eyes say that it's really true. She's on her way. And I thought it was finished . . . There are so many things between Maia and me! Those slow days in the forest, those pink moonrises over the heather, at Montigny . . . We sensed unusual things together, without speaking. When one has her eyes, the being that they've touched once is softly burned forever, I have her eyes upon me, they touch my skin, I don't really know whether she's dead or alive, whether she exits or whether she has become my dream. Love has no need of life, but only the illusion, and it extends like a taciturn lake over the infinite silence of our thought, doesn't it, Luc? We only love that illusion in others . . ."

"Listen," I said. "Someone rang the bell downstairs."

We had risen to our feet. And suddenly, Maxime gripped me and dragged me to the back of the room, away from the door, and hid behind me, leaning on the wall as if to plunge into it forever, and I heard his teeth chattering, uttering staccato words.

"Don't leave me, I beg you, you're my friend, stay . . . I'm scared . . . She's coming . . . I don't want to, I detest her, I'm afraid of her . . . I beg you, Luc . . . . Oh, the noise of the doors . . . She's coming in, coming triumphantly, she's sure of capturing me with a glance, I'm so miserable . . ."

The door opened and Maia Reni came in, hesitantly, lost in dark furs, under a thick veil behind which her celebrated eyes scintillated vaguely. She held out her hand to him, and stammered: "Maxime, it's me, my love . . ."

Her voice was as if broken, incomparably soft. She and her sad lover looked at one another. And now he was no longer afraid, and considered her ecstatically, ready to die. She came to him, divine, like a sister of exile, like a glad phantom, her light feet treading the symbolic leaflets of the carpet, the dead baneful vegetation of the past . . .

But one of Maia's movements caused the top of her mantle to part; beneath the red-tinted golden hair her diaphanous neck appeared, and a slender necklace glinted, strung with opals and aquamarines, dotted with bloody rubies . . . and the neckline of her dress, in green and pink satin, embroidered with silver anemones and forget-me-nots . . .

Involuntarily, I looked at the pastel, where the severed head was smiling among the same flowers and jewels, enigmatically.

And as I brought my gaze back to Maxime, I saw his large eyes wide open, contemplating the drops of blood pearled by the rubies on the flesh of Maia the Victorious, and I read in their indescribable expressions that she was no longer a pardoned mistress but a being much higher and more terrible, the very image and the dream of his desire, which he loved beyond her flesh and themselves, as he had loved the martyrized head of the hallucinatory pastel, and which he adored uniquely for that double and tenebrous beauty of temptation and death, as one loves through perishable forms the eternal unreality of a dream, veritably beyond life.

The Song of the Eyes

IRÈNE said to me: "Sing me the eyes. Tell me what you know about eyes. See, I'm lowering the shade over the lamp, set very low, so that our faces will be above the light and our pupils can meet without knowing one another. Tell me the eyes."

"You want the eyes, Irène? Here they are.

"Have you ever thought about gazes that descend, about those that rise, those that grip you from in front, those that slide obliquely, those that persist horizontally?

"There are the fresh eyes of women in summer, when, seated at some table at the corner of a populous street, the pensive man sees the ray of the setting sun iridescent in his absinthe, while at the end of the avenue, among the dusty crown of chestnut trees and acacias the warm scintillation of the multicolored dusk descends in glory. The fresh eyes of the women brush the pensive man, provocative, interrogative, divining, responding, while he is dreaming, his head empty and vaporous, undulating with the crowd. And the magnetism of the fugitive eyes hallucinates him.

"There are the eyes of women at diamantine and dazzling windows, and those eyes incessantly break like luminous butterflies on the pale glass in the depths of which, like a calm aquarium, strange beasts of precious stones sleep in the velvet algae, which the blow of a fist would set free, and which timid fingers do not touch. And the eyes that have gazed all day and all evening are so intense that there is no doubt that it is the very soul of their moist clarity that is fixed in those jewel-cases—and every diamond is doubled by a desirous gaze, and the diamonds also, bored by their crystal jail, desire the throat and the fine ears and the long hands of those who are contemplating them.

"There are the eyes of slightly faded women, who, half-turning while pinching the neck— delicate pleats design the torsion of the nape— gaze at young svelte people who are smoking and smiling. Gazes charged with swooning thoughts, you are like cherished gardens in autumn, and all my soul abandons itself to you, and understands you, and sympathizes with your doubt, and lights up for you with belated charity and a penetrating amour! They are faded and extinct eyes in which taciturn lust ripples; they know, they savor, they warm their lashes in odorous landscapes of flesh dormant under fatigued suns. Waiting colors them with violet mourning or verdant hope, the voluptuous cloud of quivering enjoyment attenuates them, and regret raises them up like a sad god when they open and attach themselves to the bright eyes of the young man, who will follow the young woman and bruise his heart thereupon. Those whom the late autumn has touched, how generously they would love the young man, softly lubricious, like slaves, and seductively docile, like children, and savant, and full-flavored!

"There are the eyes of the woman who is going away, amid the tumult of the railway station, where electric fruits hang from iron foliage at the tops of the arches, the edges of the hall, over the ground and the black multitude, amid the vapors, hiding the fall of night. The red signal alternates with the gold signal under the illuminated maps; carts roll thunderously; the odor of exile and smoke is intoxicating and special. The beloved is pale beneath the poorly lifted violet, the traveling mantle hiding her dear body, and in the shadow the red mouth still wants all the kisses. The descending tears mingle bitterness and adieu and, leaning over a hand that hangs down outside the window, her lover shivers. And it's necessary that she shouldn't go, it's necessary that she hurtles out of the fatal carriage and deserts with him the sinister hall, to throw herself with him across the great dark city to the closed room where one is naked without anyone coming. But a mechanical cry springs forth with anguish, the slow glide of the train increases with every passing second the distance between the man left on the platform and the frame in which the sweet face of the exile pales, and the immobile and magnetic eyes dissolve into the brutality of life.

"There are the eyes of the widow who desires and is afraid, in the morning at the cemetery, when the odor of fresh earth rises up with sensuality, in the midst of gravestones, toward the budding trees obedient to the immodest spring. The widow is young; if one were to lift up her black skirts, if one were to open her black corsage, one would find white breasts that love lips, white loins that love the embrace, long fine white legs that love the friction of a man, and that from which the aroma of amour is born. Who will pass and who will touch the body that has not renounced? Who will mingle voluptuousness with the sadness in those eyes, to evoke the lusts of the one who is dead in the bosom of new secret couplings? Above the grave the foliage and the flowers salute the new season, and the eyes of the widow slowly turn away from the ground to go toward them, hoping, being afraid . . .

"There are the eyes of little girls who, when stormy rain has fallen and the sidewalks are shiny, at six o'clock, feel an obscure fraternity in their virginal body, enervated by the damp sky, with the sumptuous prostitutes passing by. They are women already, and, although ignorant of the matters of man and woman, their little white foreheads beneath smooth tresses meditate hesitant and ardent dreams whose unreality is frightening. If their gazes are sometimes raised to look at the passers-by, they hasten those dreams and are frightened, so transparent is the armed and voracious soul therein, so forcefully does the demon of the kiss reign therein, smiling with certainty. For the soul of little girls is his kingdom, and old men know it.

"There are the placid and circled eyes of the woman who is coming back from her lover's house, and for whom caresses, by virtue of having had so much savor, will have no more before the following evening. Those eyes live on memory and refuse other eyes; they also sometimes, with a bright gleam, dispute with other eyes the joys that they have just known to the point of extenuation. Their immodest refusal and their sudden confession excite more than one offer from others; one would like to . . . but they defend themselves with a single inclination of the lashes, and the blue-tinted eyelids veil them, while slowly, still undulating with the final spasm, penetrated by perfumes, the woman passes by.

"There are eyes that have wept, those that have seen dreams of drunkenness and terror, those that have sought without finding, those that have desired without obtaining, those in which anger has shone, those that have wandered over the landscape of amour and chagrin, those in which an unhealthy flame ignites, those that youth seizes, those that are as dry and transparent as a jewel, those that bathe in the sweet water of unconsciousness, those that attach themselves and those that flee, those that resemble an infantile dawn and those that are nuanced by the sulfurous firmament of storms, those that are eternally virginal and those that seem always to have been prostituted, those that hallucinate everything that is attainable, those that go astray in the amour of the invisible, those that penetrate and those that turn away, those that yield a soul in a single glance and those that are never persuaded, those that come from the Orient, still silky with a reflection of azure and palms, and those that bear in cities the memory of northern seas, those that are sanded with gold and those that are veined like the stones of the hidden earth, those that drink life itself through the avid fascination of their shining ogives, and those that meditate obscurely, beneath the inclined curve of amorous lashes, the play of light on flesh and the play of darkness on souls . . .

"I love them all, and I wish that my eyes could contain them all in their passion, their heroism, their cynicism and their charm. I savor them; they are the rejuvenated fruits of my soul weighed down by autumn; I understand them and I love them. They are the artificial stars of the interior sky that I have constructed within myself, in order to dream there in the hours in which the veritable sky frightens me. I have an infinite mercy, tenderness and gratitude for them; thanks to them, I can live; they ornament with their trembling fires the monotony of my route; I am the friend they do not know, the confidant that awaits them, the clairvoyant and melancholy witness of their dreams. I love eyes as I love everything that is alive, I love their messages, their confessions, their pride, their refusals; I possess them, I enjoy them, I relax therein, I reflect myself therein, I am a king therein. Irène, I have spoken the song of the eyes. Irène, I have spoken the song for which you asked."

"There are other eyes yet, my love," she said. "There are mine."

And as I leaned forward without replying, to touch her eyelids with my lips, she took my head between her hands like a cup, and caused it to deviate slightly, and set her mouth on mine; and just as our mouths were about to unite, she murmured, in a feverish and low voice:

"Don't look at my eyes, lover of my soul, don't look at my eyes, or you'll steal them with your own, with your voracious eyes that almost frighten me. Here are my lips that are for you; here is my entire body, which is yours; kiss me, having spoken of what you see; kiss me, without seeing me, and savor me in obscurity."

A Fragment on Salome

THE most decisive actions of women originate far more from the hereditary soul of their race than their own personality, so it matters little whether they are anonymous or whether some veridical document remains in their regard. Powerful male wills have been reduced to nothing by courtesans whose names we shall never know, and of whom the description of their faces shows us nothing different from other women whose beauty fortified other men. We know almost nothing about women that relates to themselves, we merely observe the effects of their advent, and that effect is similar everywhere and is revealed identically in all times with a surprising force of coincidence. Women are not manifest individually because, since the commencement of societies, humans have preserved that mode, but they are manifest collectively with a terrible regularity. Their race intervenes in ours almost anonymously, and the few heroines that legend or history engages us to make into the leaders of those invasions use almost identical means with an almost invariable method.

To the seduction by the flesh and the eyes, the artful charm of the voice, the destroyer of men adds something virile and martial. Woman easily touches the blade. The gleam of bronze accomplishes that which the gleam of the gaze cannot. Helen does not fear the tumult at the Scaean Gate, and delights in the immense slaughter that takes place around Troy, the Scamander and the sea. Judith, with a backward sweep of the heavy sword, cuts off her lover's head in the darkness, and contemplates the spasm of death after that of amour. Jahel, without paling, drives a long nail with a sure hand into the temple of the sleeping Sisara. Delilah's scissors are sinister and hypocritical. Thomyris personally plunges the face of Cyrus into a vat of blood. Fredegund with the venomous eyes almost held herself the blade that killed Praetextatus. Christine of Sweden and Catherine de' Medici listened to Monaldeschi or Guise being struck down, and Elizabeth of England also loved the sharp blades that caused life to spring forth with a scream in a red flood, and the race of murderesses is perhaps even more numerous still than the taciturn horde of poisoners. Murder, and its tragic sister, complete the embrace and the moisture of the kiss, and if the woman does not strike with her own hand, the sword is always close by, and on the lips that have touched hers, the taste of death is evident.

Salome, like the others and perhaps more, evokes simultaneously the anonymous character and the bloody character. We know that the torturer stands nearby in the shadows, but we do not know exactly who she was. A few words of St. Matthew and St. Mark, and ambiguous reflections by Flavius Josephus, feebly illuminate around her the great night of history, and she appears to us as legendary as Helen or Jahel, in a time when real memories abound, in full Roman domination, under the most careful, the most documentary and the most logical administration there ever was. It seems that people did not want to talk about Salome, it seems that she appeared unimportant, like a thousand Oriental women in whom the love of lust and blood was not astonishing. Her extraordinary action left no trace. The killer of the prophet of the most considerable religion that has appeared in the world is infinitely less well-known than twenty assassins of secondary kings. That is because it does not so much reveal a personal will as manifest the collective and eternal instinct of woman. She is so perfectly feminine that she has no need to exist in herself. History is no more occupied with her than with others.

History is made for men, and what concerns women is legend. We only have legend to define their race; we illuminate the work of the race at distant intervals by means of a few terrible or adorable glimmers of light on faces that seem higher than the others, but in reality they are not higher, for all women proceed in the same fashion and obey analogous impulses. The actions of men are differentiated, and their biographies can be constituted; those of women are immutably simple, and there is no reason to talk about one rather than another. It is hazard that decides that, and that is why history intervenes awkwardly. Life is full of Fredegunds and Delilahs; we have all sensed Salome or Helen in our relationships of chance, and the most fleeting of our lovers contains, potentially, everything that makes the cynical or somber grandeur of those heroines, and if we have not, on certain sweet evenings, rediscovered Beatrice or Laure, and the luminous grace of their smile in the confident person who swoons against us, it is because our soul has not awakened with a sufficiently intuitive beauty, and we are unable to discover at that moment what is always in all of them, and eternally ready to bloom.

Thus, Salome lives in legend. And although the publican's tablet, encumbered by the numeration of the arsenals of Machaerus, was not wide enough to note down any vertical reflection in her regard, the shadow of the tragic little dancer has extended behind her through the centuries an immense series of dreams that impose themselves on the most dissimilar minds. The obscene statuette of the portal of Rouen opposes that of the patricienne of Luini, the cold child princess of Memlinck or the undulating young woman of Quentyn Massys. Flaubert remembered her in order to write the most lapidary of his tales. Rochegrosse fixes her in an exact sunlit and barbaric vision, Gustave Moreau stands her up in hectic gemstones, Oscar Wilde makes her a strange incantatrice who murmurs the sumptuous obscenity of her dreams to the pure martyr, Stéphane Mallarmé renders her prophetic in perhaps the purest fragment of poetry that our language possesses, Jules Laforgue modernizes her with a laughing and cruel genius. All those who have leaned anxiously over the mysterious motives that impel women know who Salome is, and even passers-by have retained her name. And yet, the real Salome is unknown and no one cares about her, to the point that she has been made into a double being and no one is sure of her person.

Herodias and Salome are often confused. The memory of the mother and that of the child have been mingled, one named for the other indifferently; the blade or the hair of the severed head are placed in one or the other hand. People neglect to observe that Herodias, aged, hated the Baptist, and, no longer counting on fading beauty to extract from Antipas the order of death, offered him her young daughter Salome as the price of blood. And that is because those two women are so narrowly united in the instinct of woman that it does not matter to anyone, in fact, that their soul was incarnated in two bodies. Their wills completing one another and fused, their persons mingled in one alone, they become whatever the caprice of the poet or painter makes them; and whether they are the Italian women of Ghirlandaio or Luini, Gustave Moreau's enchantress or Oscar Wilde's Jewess, they remain true, with the essential verity of legends, by virtue of the essential gesture: the one that summons the executioner from behind the shadowy door. In this case the interpretation is legitimate in all the fantasies. It is sufficient for the name of Herodias to appear more sonorous and grandiloquently

Oriental for poets to have preferred it to that of Salome; the two names have been able to designate the mother and the daughter, but they really only design a single being—and that being is also called Delilah, or Judith, or Balkis, or anything one wishes, for there is a series of masks that one hooks at one's whim over the visage and the fatality of woman.

The psychology of Salome varies in accordance with those who treat it, and yet it is frightfully simple. Herodias' resentment against the prophet's anathemas, Antipas' drunkenness, the sudden lust that decides him, all constitutes a separate political drama. Salome herself is a very beautiful child; she has only to appear for desire and death to rise up to her left and right without her having wished it. For the work of life is infallibly balanced by a work of destruction, and that unbreakable law weighs down on the little head of the lisping and joyful girl. Some, violating history, and even legend, with beauty, have supposed Salome to be amorous of St. John, and make her kill him to avenge her refusal.

In Stéphane Mallarmé's poem, Salome—or rather Herodias, since he names her thus deliberately—quivers in expectation of "something unknown." And it seems that the poet has, indeed, seen in her the soul of the ancient Orient, frightened by the prescience of a new world and a new faith in the apostle's violent words. It seems that she goes, weary of voluptuousness, toward that chaste revelator of different consciousness and an unforeseen fatalism. In Oscar Wilde's drama Salome is merely the imperious and cynical barbarian child who wants to kiss the mouth of the pure man, and who, not having had it alive, will kiss it dead amid the blood of the golden basin. Those are strange dreams.

Others see in the murderous dancer the permanent symbol of fatal grace, of eternal impure beauty assassinating thought. For them, Salome is the chimerical being, the dancer-flower, the unconscious butterfly who dances above life like the phantom of folly, illuminating and hallucinating a brain, and then leaving it in the despairing darkness. And that one is seen in poets as well as thinkers. And I remember that one evening, Loie Fuller, interpreting the subject at the Nouveau-Théâtre, gave me a striking intuition, a vision close to my heart.

Heavy with a lascivious and very real flesh, odorous and slothful, a Jewess appeared, almost a daughter of an Oriental hovel, brought up on the mats of some bazaar, with round and full breasts and palpable hips—the only one there not made of gilded paper—bargaining against the shaggy head plastered with red clots a true prostitute's musculature among the warm odor of meat and aromatics. Comprehensively, the artiste, whom one expected to be dainty and powdered, had sensed that it was necessary to be violently real, that the game around a severed head could not be different, that the blood should not be parodic, and the horror, like the tetrarch's desire, ought here to break with theatrical convention and spurt forth!

People scarcely understood; the genius of that materiality was disconcerting; it could not be admitted that Salome, the procuress of the executioner, might be neither spick and span nor very pretty, nor decked in gems. And there remain from that a few exquisite gypsographic prints,[1] and sure, sharp and gripping drawings by Pierre Roche, who did understand Loie . . .

1 It does not appear that any photographic prints survive today of Loie Fuller's representations of Salome in Paris in the early 1890s, although advertising posters do. There is, however, one print from a 1907 performance reproduced on the world wide web, which shows the heavily-built dancer in that role, with her hands on her hips, which presumably preserves the impression that seized Mauclair. Sculptures by Pierre Roche also survive—along with depictions by other adherents of Art Nouveau—but inevitably romanticize the subject; the most famous one dates from 1901, so Mauclair could only have seen the sketches on which it was based when he wrote this article.

But if I think of Salome I cannot even think of so many things. She is simple; she is simple, and she is terrible because she is simple. She leaves us brutally in the presence of a tragic fact, because she is like all women, because she does not know what she is accomplishing, because she only thinks about the minute in which she is living, because she has been asked to dance, because she knows how to dance, because she likes dancing—and she dances, and that is all! And that is sufficient for everything to happen, for maternal hatred to be satisfied, for the king to be pitiless, for the captive genius to be crushed, and for the centuries to be astonished.

She is simple, Salome. She is a little girl. She is not amorous of the prophet, she is not aveng-ing herself, she does not know what she is going to cause, she is not thinking of anything intel-lectual. Someone says to her: "Dance, Salome," and she dances, since she has learned. And that amuses her, and she is naturally immodest, and the eyes of men do not intimidate her. That eve-ning, she dances as she often does, there is noth-ing exceptional about it; why should she suspect that anything is going to happen? She sees the executioner, but he is always present. And if, this time, the dance and the immodesty decree the decapitation of the annunciator of a world, little Salome knows nothing about it.

What is extraordinary is that the child, with her nascent breasts and her shrill laughter, is suddenly invested with the eternal power of woman. She has been told to play, she plays. Women play because they are frivolous and the little girl always lives within them. This one plays like the others. And when she advances toward the tetrarch, swaying her hips, and when she pronounces the words Herodias has whispered to her: "I want you to give me the head of John the Baptist," she hesitates, she is embarrassed, she does not know exactly why she is being made to ask for that, she is almost sulky because she would rather have asked for something else for her own pleasure. The prophet's head is not for her; Salome does not know. The eternal soul of the woman of amour and blood has passed into her through her mother's mouth, poor little instrument of fatality, and her body has served uniquely to incarnate that soul, and everything that results therefrom does not concern her.

She scarcely exists, Salome, she exists just enough to be pretty and to sow death. Why are you astonished that nothing is known about her, that she has even been confused with her mother? She is of no great interest, after all. She

is like all the others, if you think about it. She is
the minuscule point of departure of a series of
immense events of which she has no suspicion.

She is, like all the others, ephemeral, as
ephemeral as those who put their lips on our lips
and in whom we stupidly believe that we are em-
bracing charity, generosity, the dream become
visible, and who will suddenly go away and leave
us in our frightful and imbecilic despair, who
will go away because they have caused what was
necessary, who go away like opium smoke after
the intoxication for which one wished has come,
who go away, go away, because they are the crea-
tures of a minute and there is no reason for them
to stay . . .

Salome passed beside St. John, she danced as
she passed, and St. John is dead, and the prophetic
sublimity has been stifled in blood, and that is
all. Why ornament fatality with more profound
and more complex motives? This one suffices for
it to be manifest in all its grandiose terror, and
our stories and commentaries are superfluous.
Salome has only one thing to do: she dances and
laughs, and everything is consummate!

And I can see nothing more troubling,
nothing that opens to us more suddenly the
doors of the terrible abysms of death, than the
unconsciousness of that little girl, *who does not*

understand what is happening, and who, in a few minutes of obscene torsion, has avenged a queen, maddened a king, and annihilated a genius, without a reason, without passion, without discernment—and she, a thin Judean dancer, is suddenly put in the balance before the divine tribunal with a prophet, removing him disdainfully from life with the negligent sway of her hips.

A PARTIAL LIST OF SNUGGLY BOOKS

LÉON BLOY *The Tarantulas' Parlor and Other Unkind Tales*

FÉLICIEN CHAMPSAUR *The Latin Orgy*

BRENDAN CONNELL *Metrophilias*

QUENTIN S. CRISP *Blue on Blue*

LADY DILKE *The Outcast Spirit and Other Stories*

BERIT ELLINGSEN *Vessel and Solsvart*

EDMOND AND JULES DE GONCOURT
Manette Salomon

RHYS HUGHES *Cloud Farming in Wales*

VICTOR JOLY *The Unknown Collaborator*
and Other Legendary Tales

BERNARD LAZARE *The Mirror of Legends*

JEAN LORRAIN *Masks in the Tapestry*

JEAN LORRAIN *Nightmares of an Ether-Drinker*

JEAN LORRAIN *The Soul-Drinker*
and Other Decadent Fantasies

CAMILLE MAUCLAIR *The Frail Soul and Other Stories*

CATULLE MENDÈS *Bluebirds*

LUIS DE MIRANDA *Who Killed the Poet?*

DAMIAN MURPHY *Daughters of Apostasy*

KRISTINE ONG MUSLIM *Butterfly Dream*

YARROW PAISLEY *Mendicant City*

DAVID RIX *A Suite in Four Windows*

FREDERICK ROLFE *An Ossuary of the North Lagoon*
and Other Stories